This edition published by Parragon Books Ltd in 2017 and distributed by

Parragon Inc.
440 Park Avenue South, 13th Floor
New York, NY 10016
www.parragon.com

This special edition was printed for Kohl's Department Stores, Inc.
(for distribution on behalf of Kohl's Cares, LLC, its wholly owned subsidiary) by Parragon, Inc.

Made in China
KOHL'S
Style Number 10598
Factory Number: 126509
9/17

Sleep Tight, Sleepy Bears

PaRragon

Bath · New York · Cologne · Melbourne · Delhi
Hong Kong · Shenzhen · Singapore

There was a **big** sleepy bear,

and a little sleepy bear.

The big sleepy bear yawned

a great big yawn,

and the little sleepy
bear yawned

a little sleepy yawn.

Then the great
big bear

gave a great big
s t r e t c h ,

and the little sleepy bear gave a little sleepy
s t r e t c h .

Then the **big** sleepy bear got into bed,

and the little sleepy bear got into bed.

Then the **big** sleepy bear put his head on the pillow,

and the little sleepy bear
put his head on the pillow.

Then the **big** sleepy bear
closed his eyes,

and the little sleepy bear closed his eyes.

Then the big sleepy bear sang

a sleepy song:

When I lay me down

to sleep,

Four bright angels

around me keep.

Two to watch me through the night.

And two to wake me come daylight.

And the little sleepy bear sang

a sleepy song:

When I lay me down
to sleep,
Four bright angels
around me keep.

Two to watch me through the night.

And two to wake me come daylight.

Softer
and
softer
and
softer.

Then the **big** sleepy bear closed his eyes,

and the little sleepy bear closed his eyes.

And the little sleepy bear
thought of the darkness,
and the starlight,

and the **big** round moon,

and how he'd be sleeping soon.

Then the **big** sleepy bear whispered, "Sleep tight."

And the little sleepy
bear didn't say
a word, because he
was sound asleep.